Tundra Books, an imprint of Penguin Random House Canada Young Readers, a Penguin Random House Company

Hampson, Sharon, author
Sharon, Lois and Bram's Skinnamarink / Sharon Hampson, Lois Lilienstein, Bram Morrison ; illustrated by Qin Leng.

Issued in print and electronic formats.
ISBN 978-0-7352-6406-9 (hardcover).–ISBN 978-0-7352-6407-6 (EPUB)

I. Lilienstein, Lois, author II. Morrison, Bram, author III. Leng, Qin, illustrator IV. Title. V. Title: Skinnamarink.

PS8615.A5455S53 2019 jC813'.6 C2018-905596-0
C2018-905597-9

Published simultaneously in the United States of America by Tundra Books of Northern New York, an imprint of Penguin Random House Canada Young Readers, a Penguin Random House Company

Library of Congress Control Number 2018959000

Acquired by Tara Walker
Edited by Elizabeth Kribs
Designed by John Martz
The artwork in this book was created with ink and watercolor.
The text was set in Burbank Small.

Printed and bound in China

www.penguinrandomhouse.ca

3 4 5 23 22 21 20 19

To all the children and families who have come together to sing "Skinnamarink"

And to Lois, who brought "Skinnamarink" from her family to ours

– S & B

For Ted and Jenna

– Q

Sharon, Lois & Bram's Skinnamarink

with Randi Hampson

illustrated by Qin Leng

tundra

We started singing "Skinnamarink" in 1978 at our very first concert, and we never stopped. Lois brought the song to us from her family and it became part of our musical family, a family that has grown from hundreds to millions. In this special book version of the song, we have added an introduction and some additional verses.

We have heard "Skinnamarink" sung by our children and grandchildren. We have heard it sung in classrooms and playgrounds and by people all over the world, even in countries where English is not the primary language. Imagine – *skinnamarink* might be someone's first English word! We have heard it sung by adults too: business people, famous entertainers, athletes, even politicians. We have heard the song at weddings to cue kissing. Over the years, it has come to symbolize friendship, joy and love.

Children, parents, grandparents, families and friends sing "Skinnamarink" to each other and sing it together loudly and proudly. We will never tire of watching families as they leave our shows happily singing it to each other.

How wonderful that something so simple can bring people together and encourage singing and loving. We hope you will read this book and help us spread this message of love.

Photo: The Canadian Press / Aaron Harris

Here's a little ditty that we all know and sing.
We share it with our families and let our voices ring.
It also has some actions that we know are fun to do.
And now we want to sing this special song with all of you . . .

Skin-na-ma-rink-y dinky dink, skin-na-ma-rink-y doo, **I love you!**

Skin-na-ma-rink-y dinky dink, skin-na-ma-rink-y doo, **I love you!**

I love you
in the morning,

and in the afternoon.

I love you in the evening,

underneath the moon.

Skinnamarinky dinky dink, skinnamarinky doo,

I love you!

I love you when you're happy,

and when you're
feeling blue.

And when you're
feeling grumpy,

I’ll give a hug to you.

Skinnamarinky dinky dink, skinnamarinky doo,

I love you!

I love you in the Arctic, the desert, by the sea . . .

. . . and on the top of the mountain standing next to me.

Skinnamarinky dinky dink, skinnamarinky doo,

I love you!

I love you
in the summer,

the fall and winter too.

I love you in the springtime.
I love you through and through.

Skinnamarinky dinky dink, skinnamarinky doo,

I love you!

Be sure to sing this love song with everyone around.

When we all sing together, it's such a lovely sound.

Skinnamarinky dinky dink,
skinnamarinky doo,

I love you!
I love your singing!
I love you!
You're all terrific!

I love you!
Let's sing together!
I LOVE YOU TOO!

Boop-boop-ee-do.

SHARON HAMPSON, the late **LOIS LILIENSTEIN** (d. 2015) and **BRAM MORRISON** are some of Canada's most famous children's performers, with fans across North America and around the world. The trio, known simply as Sharon, Lois and Bram, formed in Toronto in 1978 and went on to create two top-rated children's television shows, *The Elephant Show* and *Skinnamarink TV*. The group released 21 full-length albums, many of which reached gold, platinum, double platinum and triple platinum. They were goodwill ambassadors for UNICEF, have won countless awards and were appointed to the Order of Canada in 2002. In 1998, they performed at the UN General Assembly, and in 1994, they performed at the annual White House Easter Egg Roll. They also performed a run at the renowned Palace Theatre on Broadway. In 2018, Sharon and Bram celebrated the 40th anniversary of the group, and they continue to entertain children and share their message of love.

ACKNOWLEDGMENTS

Working on this book was a collaborative process. The vision for it would never have been realized without the significant participation of Jennifer Mitchell of Casablanca Kids and Randi Hampson who together spearheaded our team. Thanks as well to Elizabeth Kribs who has been so patient, understanding and supportive of this creative experience, which resulted in a book we are so proud of. And a special thanks to Qin for conveying the joy at the heart of this song through her beautiful artwork.

QIN LENG has illustrated picture books, magazines and book covers with publishers around the world. Recent picture books include her author/illustrator debut *I Am Small*; *Ordinary, Extraordinary Jane Austen* written by Deborah Hopkinson; and *A Family Is a Family Is a Family* written by Sara O'Leary. *Hana Hashimoto, Sixth Violin*, written by Chieri Uegaki, was a finalist for the Governor General's Literary Award, and received the APALA Award for best picture book. She lives in Toronto, with her husband and her son. Find out more at www.qinillustrations.com.